j 551.22
G289e

11/01

DU)

NATURAL DISASTERS
AN IMAGINATION LIBRARY SERIES

EARTHQUAKES

by Victor Gentle and Janet Perry

Gareth Stevens Publishing
A WORLD ALMANAC EDUCATION GROUP COMPANY

Please visit our web site at: www.garethstevens.com
For a free color catalog describing Gareth Stevens' list of high-quality books and
multimedia programs, call 1-800-542-2595 (USA) or 1-800-461-9120 (Canada).
Gareth Stevens Publishing's Fax: (414) 332-3567.

Library of Congress Cataloging-in-Publication Data

Gentle, Victor.
    Earthquakes / by Victor Gentle and Janet Perry.
        p. cm. — (Natural disasters: an imagination library series)
        Includes bibliographical references and index.
        ISBN 0-8368-2832-1 (lib. bdg.)
        1. Earthquakes—Juvenile literature. [1. Earthquakes.]
    I. Perry, Janet, 1960- II. Title. III. Series.
    QE521.3.G43   2001
    551.22—dc21   00-051621

First published in 2001 by
Gareth Stevens Publishing
A World Almanac Education Group Company
330 West Olive Street, Suite 100
Milwaukee, WI 53212 USA

Text: Victor Gentle and Janet Perry
Page layout: Victor Gentle, Janet Perry, and Joel Bucaro
Cover design: Joel Bucaro
Series editors: Mary Dykstra, Katherine Meitner
Picture researcher: Diane Laska-Swanke

Photo credits: Cover, pp. 5, 9, 13, 15 © AP/Wide World Photos; pp. 7, 21 © Mark Downey/
Lucid Images; p. 11 U.S. Department of the Interior, U.S. Geological Survey; p. 17 © Mark E.
Gibson/Visuals Unlimited; p. 19 R. E. Wallace/U.S. Geological Survey

Printed in the United States of America

1 2 3 4 5 6 7 8 9 05 04 03 02 01

Front cover: *October 1, 1995: a large quake hit the Turkish town
of Dinar. Half of the buildings collapsed, killing more than sixty
people. Specially designed buildings could have saved many lives.*

TABLE OF CONTENTS

Words that appear in the glossary are printed in **boldface** type the first time they occur in the text.

DEADLY EARTHQUAKES

Disaster struck Taiwan, an island off the coast of China, on the morning of September 21, 1999. The next day, two more strong **tremors** hit. The ground split. Buildings toppled. Dams burst. Bridges collapsed. Roads were ripped apart. It was a violent and deadly series of earthquakes. Nearly 2,300 people died, and more than 8,000 people were injured.

The worst earthquake of the century, however, hit mainland China in 1976. In Tangshan, a massive earthquake tore through the city and the surrounding countryside in northeast China. More than a quarter of a million people died. A disaster this big is hard to imagine.

Rescue workers and firefighters search for victims in the rubble of a hotel in Taipei, Taiwan. The hotel toppled during the earthquakes that hit the island in 1999.

EARTHQUAKES BIG & SMALL

More than a million earthquakes are detected each year. Only a few are violent enough to cause serious destruction and kill people.

Earthquakes can last from just a few seconds to a few minutes. Most earthquakes are very small and can only be detected by scientific instruments. You can't feel them at all. Slightly stronger ones might rumble like a heavy truck going by on a bumpy road.

Even stronger earthquakes shake the ground hard, knocking buildings and people down. Worse ones cause the ground to heave, split, or slide. Large areas of ground can rise up or sink. Coastal sections of land might even disappear under the sea.

The ground opened up near a home in San Francisco, California, during a strong earthquake in October 1989. The quake wrecked buildings and highways, killing 68 people.

THE RICHTER SCALE

Earthquakes are measured on a machine called a **seismograph**. A pen attached to a spring traces wavy lines on a piece of paper to record the ground shaking. Taller waves show bigger movements.

The size, or **magnitude**, of an earthquake is measured using the **Richter scale**. An American earthquake scientist, or **seismologist**, Charles F. Richter, created this scale in 1935. The Richter scale is based on the waves traced on a seismograph.

Each whole number in the Richter scale indicates an earthquake ten times stronger than the next lower number. So a Magnitude 5.0 (M5.0) earthquake is ten times stronger than an M4.0. An M7.0 is a hundred times stronger than an M5.0. The Tangshan earthquake in China was an M8.0.

8

A neighborhood in the Turkish town of Duzce on November 13, 1999, after an M7.2 earthquake damaged hundreds of buildings and killed more than 300 people.

THE PRESSURE BUILDS

Earth's outer shell is broken up into giant slabs, like pieces of a huge jigsaw puzzle. These slabs, called **tectonic plates**, make up large pieces of continents or the ocean floor. Ever so slowly, these giant pieces are always moving and changing shape. They never quite fit together.

Each year, the plates move about as fast as your fingernails grow — about 3 inches (7.5 centimeters). They scrunch together, slip-slide against each other, or move apart as new plates are formed from molten rock under the ocean floor or beneath the ground.

Plates don't scrunch or slide smoothly. Pressure builds up in the rocks, sometimes over many years, until a breaking point is reached. Then, the ground suddenly moves: the Earth quakes.

Earth's ocean floor and landmasses are broken up into giant tectonic plates, seven really big ones and eight to thirteen smaller ones, each growing or shrinking as they move.

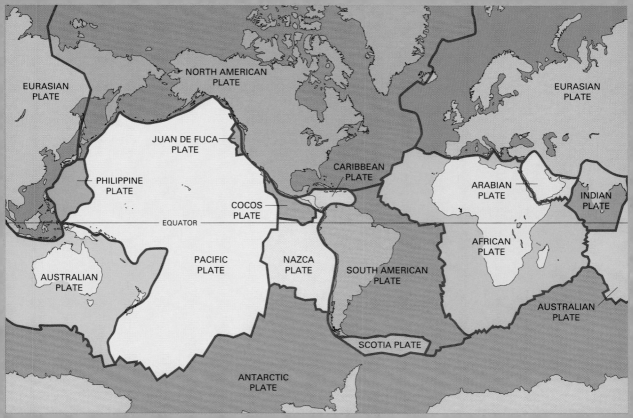

EARTHQUAKES & VOLCANOES

Earthquakes usually happen when one tectonic plate meets another. Plates push alongside or into each other. Huge pressure builds, but there is no movement. Suddenly, the pressure is too great. The plates slide against each other, or one plate forces another deeper into the ground. These sudden movements are earthquakes.

The same forces that cause earthquakes can also create **volcanoes**. When a plate is forced deep into the ground, the rock heats up and sometimes melts. The molten rock can force its way to the surface and make a volcano. An earthquake can even weaken the surface rock above an underground pool of molten rock and trigger a volcanic eruption.

The 1995 M7.2 earthquake in Kobe was the deadliest in Japan since 1923. More than 6,000 people died. Here, a bus barely escapes plunging off a collapsed freeway.

TSUNAMI!

When an earthquake takes place under the sea, the result is often a **tsunami** — a giant wave. If you punch the side of a filled inflatable pool, you will see a similar effect. Waves will travel across the water's surface.

Tsunamis can speed across oceans quickly, sometimes as fast as 600 miles (965 kilometers) per hour — the speed of a jet! They can make huge waves as they come to shore. Tsunamis can be as high as 100 feet (30 meters) by the time they crash into land.

An earthquake in one part of the world can set up a tsunami that destroys a coastal village half a world away, only a few hours later.

14

A quake under the Sea of Japan shook the islands of Hokkaido and Okushiri. Within minutes, a tsunami appeared. The waves smashed buildings and boats.

PREDICTING QUAKES

If you have enough warning, you can escape an earthquake. But some earthquakes don't give any warning. The Tangshan earthquake of 1976 was a deadly surprise.

In 1975, the people living in Haicheng, China, were luckier. Scientists began to worry that a big quake would hit this area soon, because more and more small tremors were being detected. Then one morning, the tremors suddenly stopped.

Scientists were concerned that this meant an earthquake was on the way, so they issued a warning. People living in Haicheng paid attention, and most left the city. A gigantic quake hit just five hours later. Nearly all of Haicheng's buildings were destroyed, but thousands of lives were saved.

Better earthquake-resistant building will help decrease damage to structures like this one, which was destroyed in a 1981 quake in California.

WARNING SIGNS?

A **fault** is formed when the ground cracks under the strain of two plates moving against each other. One of the most famous faults is the 750-mile (1,200-km) San Andreas Fault, found along the coast of California.

Seismologists have studied the San Andreas Fault and many smaller faults that crisscross it for years. These scientists have traced thousands of years of earthquake history. They know which parts of the fault system will most likely get big earthquakes in the next hundred years. But when? They are not sure.

Some earthquakes seem to give warning signs: small tremors sometimes hit before large ones. However, we still can't predict for sure if a big quake will happen in a few days or even in a few hours.

The San Andreas Fault slices through two-thirds of the length of California. Rivers, and roads, too, have been split apart by the sideways sliding.

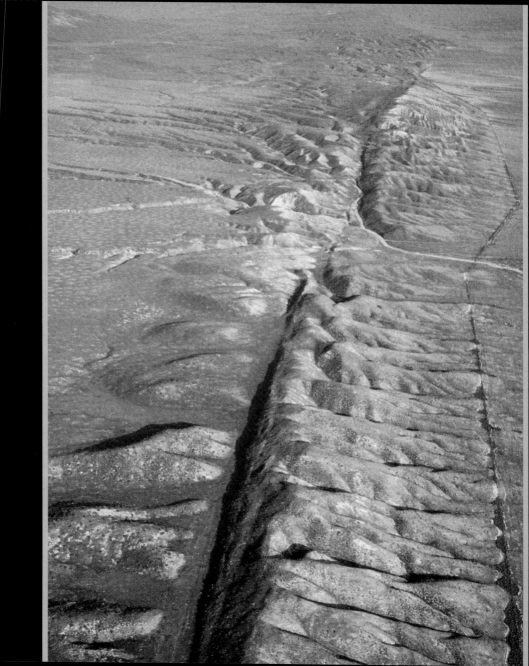

BUILDING AND PREDICTING

The best way to prepare for earthquakes is to avoid building homes, offices, factories, dams, or bridges on or near fault lines. If people must build in high-risk areas, it is important to build earthquake-resistant buildings.

Stiff, rigid buildings are often shaken to pieces in an earthquake. More flexible buildings can sometimes survive being rocked, especially if the architects designing the buildings understand how a typical local earthquake shakes the ground.

We can reduce the damage and loss of life by learning how to predict earthquakes better and how to build stronger buildings.

Construction workers examine the damage to a raised highway after the M7.1 earthquake that hit San Francisco in 1989.

MORE TO READ AND VIEW

Books (Nonfiction)   *Ask Isaac Asimov* (series). (Gareth Stevens)
Atlas of Earth. Alexa Stace (Gareth Stevens)
Earthquake: The Violent Earth. John Dudman (Thomson Learning)
Earthquake: The World Reacts. Paul Bennett (Smart Apple)
Earthquakes. Allison Lassieur (Capstone)
Earthquakes. Sally M. Walker (Carolrhoda)
Earthquakes and Tsunamis (Associated Press Library of Disasters).
   Robin Doak (Grolier)
Easy-Read Fact Book: Earthquakes. David Lambert (Franklin Watts)
San Francisco Earthquake, 1989 (Death and Destruction). Victoria
   Sherrow (Enslow)
Volcano and Earthquake. Susanna Van Rose (Dorling Kindersley)
Volcanoes (Natural Disasters). Victor Gentle and Janet Perry
   (Gareth Stevens)
World Almanac for Kids. Elaine Israel (World Almanac Books)

Books (Fiction)   *Earthquake at Dawn.* Kristiana Gregory (Gulliver/Harcourt Brace)
Earthquake Terror. Peg Kehret (Puffin)

Videos (Nonfiction)   *The Day the Earth Shook.* (WGBH/NOVA)
Earthquake. (WGBH/NOVA)
Killer Quake! (WGBH Boston)
RRReal Earthquakes. (Brentwood)

Videos (Fiction)   *Aftershock.* (Hallmark)
Earthquake. (Goodtimes)

WEB SITES

If you have your own computer and Internet access, great! If not, most libraries have Internet access. The Internet changes every day, and web sites come and go. We believe the sites we recommend here are likely to last and give the best and most appropriate links for our readers to pursue their interest in earthquakes, volcanoes, tsunamis, plate tectonics, and geoscience.

www.ajkids.com

Ask Jeeves Kids. Here's a great research tool.
Some questions to try out in Ask Jeeves Kids:
*Where can I find a map of tectonic
plate zones?*
*How many people live within ten miles
(16 km) of the San Andreas fault?*
*What museums have online earthquake
exhibits?*

You can also just type in words and phrases with "?" at the end, for example,
Magma? Volcanos?

www.crustal.ucsb.edu/ics/understanding

Understanding Earthquakes. This site has a great earthquakes quiz, an animated rotating globe showing where earthquakes happen, other interesting animations, and a good list of links.

www.leightongeo.com/Slideshows.htm

The 1999 Taiwan Earthquake. A remarkable slide show made by Dr. Bruce R. Clark, President of Leighton and Associates, Inc., during his recent visit to Taiwan. Dr. Clark was checking out the damage caused by the September 21, 1999, earthquake.

www.sfmuseum.org/1906/06.html

The 1906 San Francisco earthquake. This site features historical information about the 1906 San Francisco earthquake, including a large selection of photographs, from the Museum of the City of San Francisco.

www.scecdc.scec.org/slidesho.html

The Southern California Earthquake Center features a slide show of the 1994 Northridge earthquake.

**www.ngdc.noaa.gov/seg/hazard/
hazards.shtml/**

Natural Hazards Databases. In addition to an amazing photo gallery (click on slide sets) of earthquakes, tsunamis, volcanoes, and other natural hazards (and the debris they leave behind), there is a series of kids' quizzes on hazards ranging from volcanoes and earthquakes to wildfires and tsunamis.

www.tsunami.org

Pacific Tsunami Museum. A cool site with many tsunami pictures. Whether a tsunami is caused by an undersea earthquake or an asteroid impact, it can be devastating to coastal areas.

GLOSSARY

You can find these words on the pages listed. Reading a word in a sentence helps you understand it even better.

fault (FAWLT) — a line along which two sections of the earth's rocks move against each other during an earthquake 18, 20

magnitude (MAG-ni-tewd) — the size of something. The Magnitude number of an earthquake is a measure of how big or how strong it is. The most violent earthquake ever recorded was a Magnitude 9.5, or "M9.5" 8

Richter scale (RIK-ter skale) — a scale invented by earthquake scientist Charles F. Richter, used to measure the strength of an earthquake 8

seismograph (SIZE-muh-graff) — a machine that measures how strong an earthquake is 8

seismologist (size-MAHL-uh-jist) — a scientist who studies earthquakes 8

tectonic plate (tek-TAHN-ik PLATE) — one of the very large slabs of rock making up the surface of Earth that carry parts of continents or ocean floor 10, 12

tremors (TREH-murz) — shakings of the ground during an earthquake 4, 16, 18

tsunami (su-NAH-me) — a giant ocean wave 14

volcanoes (vahl-KAY-nose) — mountains, small hills, cracks in the ground, or other areas where molten rock from beneath the ground forces its way up, sometimes explosively 12

INDEX